SHIRLEY SIATON

FOUR SHORT STORIES

Pieces of Love
Four Short Stories

Copyright © 2025 Shirley Siaton Parabia

ALL RIGHTS RESERVED.
No part of this book may be reproduced or used in any manner without the prior written permission of the copyright owner, except for the use of brief quotations in a book review. To request permission, contact the publisher at books@inkysword.com.

This is a work of fiction. Names, characters, businesses, events and incidents are the products of the author's imagination. Any resemblance to actual persons, living or dead, or actual events is purely coincidental.

All brand and product names used in this book are trademarks, registered trademarks, or trade names of their respective owners. Inky Sword Book Publishing is not associated with any product or vendor in this book.

ISBN 978-621-8371-56-9 (paperback)
First Edition, January 2025

Published by Shirley S. Parabia
Cover by Artscandare Book Design
Interior formatting by Haelah Rice Covers

Inky Sword Book Publishing
Barangay Quezon, Arevalo, Iloilo City 5000
Republic of the Philippines
inkysword.com

Warnings for references to sex and violence.

Recommended for mature readers 18 years old and above.

Dedication

To those who believe in love

In all its faces and phases

CONTENTS

Acknowledgments	ix
PART I **FIRES**	
Fires	3
Foreword	5
The Story	7
PART II **LEAVING THE MOUNTAIN**	
Leaving the Mountain	19
Foreword	21
The Story	23
PART III **RIVALS**	
Rivals	37
Foreword	39
Rivals	41
PART IV **DANCING IN THE RAIN**	
Dancing in the Rain	61
Foreword	63
The Story	65
About the Author	79
On the Web	81

Acknowledgments

I am very grateful to *MOD Filipina Magazine* for taking a chance on an unknown kid and giving her short stories the opportunity to be read the world over.

Fires

FIRES

She had been wading through dangerous waters earlier; she was now treading the deep end.

He was not supposed to be there, with her. He was not supposed to be this real, not anymore.

She thought he had gone on to live his life without her in it, just like everyone else had.

Foreword

I wrote this little love story when I was in high school, as a sort of gift to my friends Rhoda and Ramon, the original names of the female and male leads.

Even before the 'friends-to-lovers' trope became the romance go-to plot device, I wanted to capture how two friends, so inseparable before, could grow and go in different directions.

This became my piece *'Fires,'* which was later republished as *'Aflame'* in my September 2023 short story collection, *Now and Forever*.

The Story

Fires

"Lissa? Something wrong?"

She shivered slightly as a gust of wind disturbed the comforting stillness of the summer evening. She closed her eyes, luxuriating in the darkness just after sunset, and felt the soothing cricket sounds wash around her. Spending time in her mother's garden, ensconced in her favorite rocking chair, had always been comforting.

"Lissa?" Russell Suarez placed a gentle hand on her arm.

Pushing an unruly strand of hair away from her face, she finally turned her attention to him. She knew he had been standing in the garden for at least five minutes, quiet and observant. She wondered if he knew what she was thinking about.

"Hi. I thought you were packing for tomorrow's flight." She managed a little smile as she stretched and got to her feet. "It leaves early. And you still have to sit through my special *Bon Voyage* breakfast. Don't forget that."

Russell, like Lissa, was a writer. That was where the similarities ended.

He was the star columnist of a big national daily, where he wrote *Man on Fire,* an opinion segment that took on current issues and events on an entirely different, if not controversial, spin. The vacation he had taken this week was one of the very rare breaks he took from his job.

If he wasn't writing his column, he was covering national and international events. The last one had been the regional economic summit, serialized in the newspaper and syndicated in other media outlets.

On the other hand, Lissa was a freelance writer and proofreader, on top of her job as an English tutor for foreign students. She stayed in her hometown and did work here and there. She occasionally got breaks from bigger publications and had several contributions in magazines.

"Your breakfast offer is something no person in his right mind would refuse." Russell's soft brown eyes twinkled. He was as handsome as a 1940s movie star, with longish black hair framing a chiseled face with what she called a 'Hispanic' profile.

"Flatterer." She quickly averted her gaze.

"What's wrong?" he insisted. The man really was more sensitive than she gave him credit for. "Is something wrong?"

"I haven't eaten much today," she admitted, allowing him a small portion of the truth. "I don't feel like having a bite, though."

He placed an arm around her shoulders. "You sure do look pale. Why don't you come to my house? I actually came over to see if you wanted to join us. My cousins are having this big feast of *lechon* and *talaba* in my honor."

"Do you mind if I stay here for a while?"

"No, not at all."

She became quiet, leaning her aching head on his shoulder.

"So, Lissa." He cleared his throat.

Curiosity made her lift her head to look at him. He couldn't meet her eyes.

"I hope you don't mind me saying," he continued, a little more quickly than his usual relaxed manner of speech, "but you've got to take care of yourself more. Your mother told me you're fond of staying up until dawn and drinking gallons of coffee."

"I work better at night. You know that." She wrapped her arms around herself and stepped away from him.

He sighed and tried to reach for her hand. She pulled it out of his reach. "We're all concerned. I suggest you take it slowly. Don't be too hard on yourself."

"I like my work." She was beginning to feel defensive.

"Easy," he said, sensing her distress, holding up his hands. "I don't want you to get mad at me for caring about you."

Caring about you.

The words registered, but she refused herself the hope in them.

Russell was her oldest friend, someone who called during special occasions and sent her chocolates, flowers, and silly cartoon cards on her birthday. His unexpected intrusion into her routine, if not downright dull, life mere days ago had certainly been unsettling. He had spent most of his time with her, endearing himself even more to her.

"Please, Lissa," he went on pleadingly. "Don't be mad."

She sighed, defeated. There was no point in picking a fight with an unwilling opponent. "I'm sorry. Migraines make me cranky."

"Don't apologize. Come here."

He put his arm around her shoulders again, this time bringing her closer. He placed a kiss on the side of her head. As far as she could remember, he had always touched and held her like a protective older brother.

They had been close since childhood. They grew up on the same street and attended the same schools until they both finished university with degrees in Mass Communications. Their mothers were as close as sisters, too; they worked in the same government office and had both been widowed at a fairly young age.

How could she even get mad at him in the first place?

In spite of how much he had outdistanced her career-wise, Russell had never once made mention of it. Earlier that week, he had read over her tentative writing ideas for one-off feature pieces and praised them sincerely. A few days later, she had found herself talking on the phone with a pleasant-sounding woman, the lifestyle editor of the same newspaper Russell wrote for.

"Please send me your pitches for articles, Miss Garcia. I was very impressed by the samples of your work Russell sent me."

As easily and as quickly as he had breezed back into her life, he had changed it, too.

She didn't know if it was for the better, though. Not if he, just as quickly and just as easily, would leave it again.

She was as cold as ice.

The Lissa he knew very well was not this detached shell of a woman who barely said a word and disappeared into herself. She was the person he had most looked forward to spending time with during his vacation, one he had fought so hard and given up two big stories for.

The past days with her had been wonderful, enough to recharge him for the next few months of relentless work and travel, ungodly hours of writing, and even one or two anonymous death threats.

Regardless of what he was going back to, Russell didn't want to leave Lissa in the state she was in. Or he damn well wouldn't leave at all.

"Why don't we go somewhere, just like old times?" He suggested, pleasantly, trying to break through that strange wall she had put up. "I don't think I can eat any more *lechon*, to be honest, not if I want to run the marathon again."

Russell felt her discomfort as she disengaged herself from him. Had he done or said something wrong? He wracked his brains, going through the events of the past week, and came up with nothing.

Lissa hesitated. "Okay. We just have to make it back before midnight, though. My mom will tell your mom, and then they will both panic. You know how they are."

"The park, then?"

"Okay. Give me a minute and I'll meet you outside." She turned and went inside the house.

Russell, shaking his head slightly, made the short trip next door to his own house. His cousins had brought over a videoke machine; they were now singing a slightly off-key version of *'Skyline Pigeon.'* A few slices of pork and empty shells remained on the dining table.

He took the keys of his mother's car and left word that he was driving out for a while. His mother had, apparently, gone out with Lissa's mother to some ladies' club meeting.

"Russell has a hot night with his girlfriend," a cousin gleefully declared on the microphone. He ran out of his own house, followed by catcalls and whistles. He made a mental note to ask his mother to ban everyone inside from ever coming back.

His face still felt hot when he spied Lissa standing outside their gate. She had changed into a new blouse and jeans, and was carrying her handbag. He quickly went into the car and backed out of the driveway before his cousins could see and tease her, too. That would probably make her mad again, and she would most likely take it out on him.

To his relief, they made it out of the neighborhood without drawing attention. They were on the coastal road within minutes.

He gave Lissa a quick sidelong glance. She was seated a little too stiffly, her eyes on the darkened highway outside her window.

"Remember where we used to take this car when we still worked for the college paper?"

She nodded, her eyes still turned away from. "To the all-night *arroz caldo* place. Too bad they had to close it down. I miss it sometimes. None one else in town makes chicken soup like that anymore."

"We'd pool our coins together sometimes and split the serving," he added.

Lissa finally looked at him with a small smile. "And split the egg. Don't forget the egg."

"Yellow for you, white for me." Up until now, he would only ever eat the white portion of an egg. It was a habit he had picked up from all those years of sharing *arroz caldo* with her.

Silence wrapped around them. Russell turned on the radio, letting soft music fill the dark car interior. A short while later, they pulled into the parking lot of the seaside park. It was one of those places where children could play on the waterfront and shutterbugs and artists alike could catch a clear, unhampered view of the sunset or sunrise.

Ever since he could drive, he and Lissa would come to the park during the unlikeliest hours of the day and write their assignments, bingeing on half-gallons of Rocky Road bought by whichever one of them had allowance left.

The park was not very busy in the late hour. There were a few groups, mostly families and couples, scattered throughout the lawn overlooking the sea. He stepped out of the car and opened the door on her side. He wanted to hold out a hand to help her, but decided against it. She had been averse to physical contact earlier. The last thing he wanted to do was push her further away into herself.

He slowly headed for the huge stone platform built next to sea, hoping she would follow. He was relieved to see her fall into step beside him.

"I wish the rest of the gang were here," Russell said, pointing out a row of swings and naming their closest classmates from university. "Bobby, Claire, Freya and Dale. They would have attacked those kiddie-sized swings already."

The remark made her considerably relax. He could see her shoulders lose some of their stiffness.

"They have kids who attack swings now," Lissa said. "I saw Bobby and his wife in Church last month. They have three kids now. What a difference a few years could make.

"Maybe more than a few," he offered.

"Has it really been that long?" Her voice was soft, distant, almost wistful. "It feels as if time moves without me sometimes. I keep on missing out on the good stuff. It's like everyone else is living their lives out there, and I'm stuck in here."

Her words stopped him in his tracks, as if he was shot in the gut.

What could he say?

More importantly, what could he do?

Lissa had stopped walking, too. They stood in silence, looking out to the sea, until he felt her hand in his.

"I'm sorry for ruining your last night at home," she declared softly. "I shouldn't have said anything. I imagine I sound as depressing as hell."

"No, you don't." Her hand felt cool, damp and delicate. "You sound very real."

"My problems are not your problems."

He turned to look at her. She was bathed in moonlight, a heartbreakingly beautiful wisp of a woman with the darkest hair, gentlest face, sharpest eyes and most honest soul he had ever known.

His Lissa.

There was only ever one answer. "I could make them mine."

LISSA'S HEART THUNDERED IN HER EARS.

She had been wading through dangerous waters earlier; she was now treading the deep end.

Russell Suarez was not supposed to be there, with her. He was supposed to be on another high-flying assignment, a familiar name on a national byline, a larger-than-life presence on a page that took no prisoners.

He was not supposed to be *this* real, not anymore.

She thought he had gone on to live his life without her in it, just like everyone else had.

"You don't know what you're saying, Russ." Lissa let his hand go and wrapped her arms around herself. This was now her default defensive reaction, to whatever it is the man in front of her made her feel.

It was a mistake agreeing to come here in the first place.

Just as he was in his writing, Russell was unforgiving. He rounded on her. "The least you could do is give me a little credit, Lissa. I do know what I'm talking about sometimes."

"You think you know anything about me?" she shot back in frustration. "That, somehow, after a week, you could make everything better?"

"Is that what you think I want to do? Change your life? Do you think I want to be some kind of self-sacrificing hero?" He stood so still but was filled with so much passion he was practically on fire with it. This was the side of him that could turn a whole tide of sentiment, the side of him that made people take notice and listen. "I couldn't change anyone's life, least of all yours."

"What do you want to do, then?" Tears began to spring in her eyes, brought on by his fiery reaction, her fears, and the ties that bound them to each other.

"I want to be a part of your life, Lissa. I want to be there when you feel you're stuck, or if you don't want to move."

"Why?" She choked out.

"You know why." His voice was so soft she could barely hear it over the sound of the waves crashing against the shore. He need not say anything more. His gaze held all the answers.

Her hands fell limply to her sides. It felt harder to keep her feet rooted to the ground. Breathing was difficult, because, in place of the cold emptiness inside her, she was filled with so much feeling, all at once.

Wonder. Disbelief. Heat.

Love.

As with all fires, it took only a single spark.

She didn't know who moved first. She only knew she was back in his arms, but this time, his lips were on hers, his hands were in her hair, and she was melting into him, the same way he was into her.

"I hope you know what you're getting yourself into," she breathed against him.

His face was fierce, as his hands were gentle on her body. "I know I'm exactly where I'm meant to be."

There it was, in his eyes, as clear and blinding as the sun burning in the midday sky. If only she had tried to look before, maybe she would have already found it.

It didn't matter now.

She had found him, and he had found her.

Leaving the Mountain

LEAVING THE MOUNTAIN

Her voice broke at the end of the song.

The closing chords finally melded back to the subdued whirring of the CD.

He buried his head in his hands.

He had let her go, for the second time.

Foreword

I wrote this short story when I was in college. As a huge basketball and music fan, I wanted to create characters from both these worlds and bring them together in a story so heartbreakingly bittersweet, with only songs to bridge the distance between them.

Thus, *Leaving the Mountain* came into being.

It had since taken the form of a lyrical, heart-rending contemporary romance, the novella *Our Love Replay* (May 2024).

THE STORY

Leaving the Mountain

Someone was with her.

Tara Galvez's hands froze on the strings of the guitar she was cradling as she sat cross-legged on the veranda railing of her grandparents' country home.

She was enjoying her valued solitude, at the same time taking the opportunity to create new music for her next album.

"You stopped playing. Did I disturb you?"

She looked over her shoulder. It was a man, a few years older than her. He was tall, with wavy black hair and the most piercing eyes she had ever seen.

"It's okay, although I wasn't expecting company." She got off her perch and carefully placed her guitar in its case.

Tara felt her heart skip a beat as his eyes crinkled up in *that* familiar smile. It was a smile she could never forget.

The years hadn't changed him much, except this time he was more muscular than his lanky college self.

"Lucas Delgado." He extended a strong, graceful hand.

'I know,' she almost replied, but stopped herself. Instead she

drew herself up and shook his hand, praying hers wasn't trembling.

"Tara Galvez."

"I know," he answered, echoing her unspoken words. He was holding on to her hand. "From college. Besides, I'm a fan. I have a copy of your new CD, *'The Earth Is My Mother.'*"

Tara was a solo musical artist, Lucas a professional basketball player. Back in college, he had been the star of the varsity team. Two years behind Lucas, Tara had never really gotten close to him; except for the fact she regularly contributed her poems to the student publication where he was the resident artist.

Both took up Business Administration, but they ended up in different fields. Lucas entered the amateur draft of the country's premier professional basketball league and got picked in the first round by one of the most popular teams.

Tara, on the other hand, had signed a contract with a recording company after a talent scout heard her perform in an open mic night of a local resto-bar.

Success stories, she thought. The world was indeed small.

She could breathe easier when he let go of her hand. She searched her mind for something to say.

"Would you like to come inside for coffee or juice or something?" She felt a little bit foolish for her lack of manners.

Lucas smiled again. "Sure. Juice would be great, thank you."

They got into conversation as soon as they entered the house. It was rather surprising how easily they opened up to each other, considering they weren't even close during their time at school.

Then again, his charisma had always captivated her.

Now that he was in front of her, in her grandparents' home, it felt like an exhilarating new beginning.

∼

TARA GALVEZ, HE REMEMBERED, WAS THE SHY, OBSCURE freshman who had first stepped into the newspaper office hesitantly. He had been inking an editorial cartoon when she'd asked him where she could leave her poem for the literary editor.

Irritated, he had replied, "Just leave it on the table. Anything else?"

She'd shaken her head. "No. Thank you." Then she had fled.

Out of curiosity, Lucas had read her poem. Moments after he'd skimmed over the opening stanza, he had hurried to the window and tried to catch another glimpse of the girl.

How could I have been so blind? Lucas now asked himself as he looked admiringly at Tara, who confidently walked about the small, sunny room preparing drinks.

"It's championship season, isn't it? Why are you here?" Tara's voice brought him back to reality.

Lucas shrugged. "The Finals of the last conference sprained both my ankles and gave me back pain. The coach wanted me to take time off for the next season. With our import, the team has a very good chance of winning."

"I don't watch much basketball these days," she said as she placed a tall glass of orange juice before him. "As you can see, there's no electricity unless you have a generator around here. And no newspapers, either."

"How often do you go into town?"

"Not often." She took a seat directly across him. "A nice old aunt visits me here on Sundays and sometimes goes with me to Mass. You know how it is with old people. Lots of concern. So, who are you staying with?"

"Carl Divinagracia. He's my manager's brother."

"He's not exactly one of my favorite people," she replied disdainfully. "Whenever he comes here, he hunts. Shoots down birds. Please can you tell him that one of these days someone's going to make him pay for what he's doing?"

That night, over dinner, Lucas told Carl, "Maria Makiling says you should quit firing at other living things in sight."

"You've met her?" Carl looked at him incredulously.

"This morning," Lucas replied. "Apparently, she doesn't like you."

Carl chuckled. "Of course she doesn't. Now what's the punchline?"

"Romina. You know her?"

"Yes."

Lucas saw the blood drain from Carl's face. Tara had told him that Romina was Carl's 'other' girlfriend in the province. He had avoided her for the past month so he could propose to his girlfriend back in Manila sometime very soon, without the 'complications.'

They resumed eating in silence.

When he finished eating, Carl spoke up. "Hey, Luke?"

"Yeah?"

"I think I'll hang up my guns for a while."

Sunrise.

Light was pushing out of the horizon in multicolored slivers. Crowing roosters could be heard from both nearby and distant farms. The air felt cool and soothing on her face.

Tara woke up knowing that Lucas was leaving for Manila today. It felt like the sun was setting down on her, engulfing her in an endless night of loneliness.

Over the past month, Lucas had visited her in the morning during his regular jog. He had even asked for help in his training. At sundown, he would usually walk up to the house again and challenge her to a friendly one-on-one game.

Inevitably, she would always win.

A few minutes later, Lucas arrived, bringing her out of her

reverie. All pumped up and breathing heavily, his wavy hair damp, Lucas was heartbreakingly handsome.

She forced a smile on her face. "So the coach really wants you for the Finals, huh?"

"My sub twisted his right wrist and broke it into three pieces. The team lacks a starting shooting guard for the Best of Seven."

"I know. Maybe I'll go stay with my aunt in town during the games so I could watch you getting beaten to a pulp by the other team."

Lucas feigned a hurt look. "Now you are sending me off with bad vibes."

"Seriously, Luke, good luck." She flashed him what she hoped was her brightest smile.

He nodded and smiled back, then looked at his watch.

"I have to go or Carl's going to have my contract terminated." He extracted a small roll of paper from the pocket of his jogging pants.

"For you," he said, almost sheepishly, as he slipped the object into her hands. "It's my own way of saying 'thank you.' For everything".

She handed him a brown paper bag in return. "I hope you'll like it. Whatever's inside."

They stared at each other uncertainly.

It was Lucas who broke the awkward silence. "You know something, Tara? I hate goodbyes."

She felt a lump in her throat. She could only nod in agreement.

"I'll see you soon, right?"

"Okay, Luke." She swallowed. Hard. "Goodbye."

Tara was surprised when he bent down to pull her into his arms and kiss her cheek. "Goodbye, Tara."

With those words, he walked away, turning for a last goodbye wave before disappearing into the tree line.

She waited until the sound of his footsteps crunching against the fallen forest leaves was gone. Her hands closed tightly around his parting gift as a lone tear slid down her cheek.

GAME SEVEN.

Only a few hours separated him from the moment of truth.

Lucas sat on the couch and stared at the white jersey with the dark-red lettering draped on the back of a chair, ready to be packed for the night's game.

Delgado. Number One.

He felt overwhelmingly guilty and miserable.

Game Six would have been a cinch if only he hadn't missed his two free throws in the last twenty seconds. The other team had then made a perfect play for a two-pointer, tying the record three to three with a narrow one-point victory.

The CD.

Where was it? Lucas had found out that the content of the brown bag from Tara was a CD, without any label. He still hadn't listened to it, feeling too emotionally raw to do so.

He opened the drawers and closets to look for it. He located the CD on top of his night table. He realized he'd always kept it close.

Kept his memento of Tara close.

Lucas played it. There was a soft whirring sound for the first half a minute. Tara's voice then came out of the speakers.

"Hi, Luke. To be honest, I don't really know what to say. That's pretty strange, isn't it? After all, I rely on my talent to mince words and things like that."

There was another pause, followed by a soft laugh. "*Gosh. What am I doing, anyway?*

There was a brief silence, then guitar chords, tentative yet melodious, began to fill the air.

"I call this song 'Leaving the Mountain.' I wrote it last night when I couldn't sleep. I was thinking of you...and, well, this is for you."

Tara began to sing.

From the quiet
I see you walk away
Morning has dawned
But it seems to me
The night is here to stay

All will just come to pass
Still here in the calm I dwell
As you leave the sleepy old mountain
To go back to the world
You know so well

HER VOICE BROKE AT THE END OF THE SONG. THE CLOSING chords finally melded back to the subdued whirring of the CD.

Lucas buried his head in his hands.

He had let her go, for the second time.

TEARS TRICKLED DOWN HER CHEEKS AS SHE READ THE NOTE FROM Lucas, opened only moments before when Tara finally mustered the courage to do so.

I'm sorry if you think I'm kidding. I'm sorry I wasn't brave enough to tell you the truth.

All I can ever think about is you, Tara. How much I need to see you every day. How much strength you give me just by being there. How much I miss you when you're not around.

Love,
Lucas

AT THE BOTTOM OF THE PAGE, TARA'S SHAKY FINGERS TRACED Lucas' caricature of himself dressed in his basketball uniform. There was an elaborate frown on the cartoon's face. It was even crying.

She looked at her watch.

Game Seven was an hour away.

Tara grabbed her phone from the living room table, grateful that the signal was strong that day. She dialed Carl's number without hesitation.

"The number you dialed is now unattended." The recording was painful to her ears.

For the next few hours, she heard the same automated response over and over. Tara watched the game on TV in panic as the scores tied at the dying seconds of the game.

Carl's phone finally picked up the call.

"Hello?" His voice was dripping with irritation. She could hear deafening screams in the background.

Carl was right in the arena, with Lucas.

"Carl, this is Tara," she said without preamble. "I need to talk to Lucas now. Please, Carl."

It took several seconds for her words to register. "Are you crazy, Tara? He's down by the courtside in the team huddle. It's the last set of time-outs. You can't possibly-"

"Could you just give the phone to Lucas, please?" Tara pleaded, realizing she was in tears. "If you do understand what love means, please help me."

He sighed heavily. "Alright, Maria Makiling. You got me. Just this once."

Lucas saw Carl making his way to the bench, waving his phone animatedly.

"It's her," Carl mouthed, gesturing to the phone.

Without a word, Lucas left the huddle and took the call.

"Tara?"

"Lucas, I-" He heard the pain in her voice. It mirrored the sensation in his chest, which pierced like a dagger.

"What is it, sweetheart?"

"Lucas... I love you."

The world seemed to stop at those three words, but Tara was still speaking urgently.

"Just shoot the ball when you get it, okay? I believe in you. I always have. I feel so stupid for not telling you anything before you left."

"I love you, too. Since college, Tara. The moment you handed over that first poem, you never once left my mind. I promise I'll see you soon—"

The phone was snatched from his grip. One of his teammates was pointing to the floor. "Let's go, Luke. Coach says we execute play four."

Lucas looked at the game clock. It was thirty seconds before the end.

This was definitely make-or-break.

The inbound was lopsided, but he still caught the ball firmly. Twelve seconds to shoot. Eight. Someone was in his line of vision. Six. The double team. Four. He found the perfect spot.

He raised his arms and flicked his wrist. The ball hit the board, then spun around the hoop. Finally, the buzzer sounded as the ball swished through the net.

Pandemonium erupted.

"Delgado, three points!" The courtside announcer's voice boomed throughout the arena.

The other team had six seconds to shoot. Five. Lucas saw the ball settle into the hands of the opposing offensive guard. Four. The dribble.

He had to block it.

The opposing guard jumped high into the air. Lucas went with him. He saw the ball make the fateful arc, in slow motion. Automatically, his right hand punched the air.

Dimly, he felt something touch his fingertips. Then a shrill buzzing noise, the sound of finality, filled his head.

"Luke 'The Nuke' Delgado blocks the shot," said the TV commentator at courtside. "And it's over! Game clock is down to zero. We have a champion!"

SOMEONE WAS WITH HER.

Tara's hand froze on the strings of the guitar she was cradling.

Now, she didn't mind being disturbed.

"You stopped playing. Am I bothering you??"

She looked over her shoulder.

"Lucas."

She uttered his name almost hesitantly, afraid he'd disappear at the merest sound.

She could not do anything but watch him walk towards her.

He stopped when he was about a foot away, dropping onto one knee.

"I came back to be with you, Tara." He took a small velvet box from his pocket and opened it to reveal a golden band with a diamond. "I hope you will grant me the honor of staying with you, forever."

She stepped closer and touched his cheek. The warmth of his skin and the smile on his lips convinced her he was real.

"Yes, I do," she said softly. "No one's leaving, Lucas. Not now, not ever."

With the mountain as their witness, he slid the ring onto her finger, stood up, and took her into his arms.

Into their forever.

Rivals

RIVALS

He had chosen her. He trusted her with his dreams and his lifeblood.

*He didn't seem the kind of man who carelessly threw words around. Did he think **more** of her?*

Her only indisputable conclusion was that she wanted more of it all. She wanted more of him.

Foreword

I wrote this short story when I was in college, way before the 'enemies-to-lovers' trope became a staple in books and films. However, I wanted to create characters who were each other's equal, in academics and sports, rather than use the opposites-attract device.

Thus, *'Rivals'* came into being. It was later republished as *'Axis'* in my September 2023 short story collection, *Now and Forever*.

It has since taken the form of a CEO/billionaire and sports contemporary romance, the novella *The Last Divide* (November 2023).

THE STORY

"You. Insult. Me."

Koreen Cisco punctuated each word deliberately as she lowered her hips to the practice mat and deftly maneuvered Royce Duran overhead.

He barely had enough time to brace his stomach and get into a quick forward roll, landing none too gracefully in a supine position. It was a miracle he made it without breaking his neck.

"I. Actually. Felt. That." He cringed as pain shot through his lower back, feeling his age now more than ever. Dimly, he was aware of other people in the gym who had momentarily paused in whatever they were doing to look their way.

"No less than you deserve," Koreen snapped back. "The next time you walk in here to challenge the Sensei, you had better come prepared."

She was grinning from ear to ear as she looked down at him. Royce watched her half in amusement, half in amazement.

Koreen barely cleared five feet. She had black hair that sported an uneven bob cut, skin with an unusual reddish-gold tone, and the strength to break his neck with probably just a flick of her tiny wrist.

It was her chocolate-brown eyes, however, that made her different from everyone else. She had cat's eyes, which could practically wound with a glance. He figured she was very capable of actually doing that, if she set her mind to it.

"I never imagined you would ever look as miserable as you do right now. You have always been my best sparring opponent, Duran. What happened to all those lightning takedowns?"

Royce smiled inwardly. Leave it to Koreen to gloat whenever she had the upper hand. The competitive relationship he shared with her was as natural to him as the sun rising in the morning. All through elementary and secondary school, they had been pitted against each other academically to the point of sharing the valedictory honors at graduation. During high school, they both took up Judo and sparred against each other regularly.

Things changed when they reached college. Royce moved to the capital to join the elite Integrated Arts and Medicine program of the country's premier state university. Koreen stayed in town to continue her studies and now taught Mathematics in the same high school they had both attended. She also became a part-time Judo instructor at their old martial arts gymnasium.

Ever the overachieving whiz kid, he had thought wryly, upon hearing about all the things she had been up to.

Royce had, admittedly, been pathetically lacking in keeping up with his training. There were barely any Judo schools in the part of Saudi Arabia where his company was based. Karate, Taekwondo and Brazilian Jiu-jitsu were undoubtedly more popular. Besides, he would actually be lucky if he had any time left to train. He had worked for the

Saudi-based transcription company the last seven years, five as the General Manager. Reporting only to the Saudi prince who owned the business, Royce had set up branches in Dubai and Pune over the years, with the Philippines as the next frontier. To date, he nearly had a thousand people in his employ.

"Well." he replied, smiling and taking the hand she extended to help himself up, "maybe all those years behind a desk has made me soft." His smile became devilish. "Or maybe not."

BEFORE HER BRAIN COULD REGISTER WHAT WAS GOING ON, Koreen found herself pinned to the mat, ballroom-dip style. His left hand was around her waist, the other braced on the surface to keep both their balance. She realized that Royce did so to spare her own back from the impact.

He had just waltzed back into the gym that very afternoon. He had done enough showing-off to last her a lifetime.

Royce Duran. Ever since they were children, he was a paragon of everything she had secretly envied. He was good-looking, effortlessly athletic, undeniably charismatic, and a natural-born leader. She relied on her smarts and the unusual amount of physical strength she was gifted with; she was a far cry from being described as an attractive girl. Competing with someone whom other people always seemed to like more had been exhausting.

His smooth brown face was very, very close to hers. Koreen felt his almost-black irises look right into her soul. The scent of him engulfed her. It was a sporty kind of cologne, understated and subtle.

Their eyes locked.

Then Royce said: "Or maybe I just got lucky." This time, he

effortlessly pulled her to her feet. "You haven't lost your touch, Koreen."

She felt the breath that she had been holding exit her lungs in a loud *whoosh*.

"You're not that bad," she said grudgingly. "Not yet, anyway."

"I should be grateful for that, I guess," he replied, as they faced each other and bowed. "Given how rusty I have apparently become."

"You should be on your way before I catch my second wind." Koreen averted her attention from him and gestured for her students to take their spots on the training mats. She was positive she heard giggles and snickers. It was, after all, a milestone to see the teacher get whipped in the ass.

"As you wish, Sensei." He bowed again and paused when she was at eye level. "I'll pick you up from school Friday afternoon. Dinner's on me, of course. The winner always picks up the tab." Royce straightened and headed for the men's locker room.

"Not on your life, Duran," she whispered, glaring at his retreating back and smoothing down the wrinkles of her white kimono.

"Ten rounds of running around the gym to warm up," she snapped at her students. Where was their loyalty to their teacher when she needed it most?

She only felt satisfied when she heard groans and protests instead.

"Excuse me, Miss Cisco?"

Koreen looked up from the stack of test papers she was grading. It was late afternoon. All the other teachers had left for the day. She was savoring a rare moment of solitude in the faculty room before going to the gym later that evening for a grueling two-hour session with her advanced class.

One of her senior students in Advanced Algebra had poked his head through the half-open doorway. He was wearing a school sports jersey, probably still at practice in the courts near her office. "Yes, Paul? How can I help you?"

"There's someone asking for you. He said he was a classmate of yours."

"He's here?" The words escaped her mouth before she could stop herself. She had completely forgotten about Royce's dinner offer.

"Hey, Paul. Is your Ma'am Cisco in there?" She heard a deeper, older male voice coming from the corridor.

Paul's head disappeared from sight. "Yup," she heard the boy say. "She's right in there, Mister Duran."

A few more words were exchanged, before she heard a set of receding footsteps.

"Good afternoon, Ma'am." It was Royce's turn to poke his head through the doorway. "Although you look more like a student, I'm getting a very strange sense of *déjà vu* right now."

Koreen glared at him "Did you come all the way here just to throw jabs at my age?"

"Actually, I came here to make good on my dinner invitation," he answered, deadpan.

"I thought you were joking." Koreen sighed and shook her head. "I honestly didn't think you meant any of it."

Royce held up his hands in what looked like mock surrender.

It was then she saw that he actually came *dressed* for dinner. His hair was gelled neatly and he was wearing a well-cut aqua-colored polo shirt and dark blue slacks. His feet were encased in what looked like black leather boots, shiny and expensive looking. He was not conventionally handsome with his sharp features, but her eyes were irresistibly drawn to his face. Laugh lines and other signs of maturity now tempered his boyish toughness, but she would be a hypocrite if she denied how attractive he really was.

"I meant what I said," he replied, with a charming grin. "I'm sorry if you thought I was trying to pull some kind of stunt on you. At our age, we should have already outgrown whatever bad blood we had between us by now."

Koreen put down her pen and pushed the papers on her desk to one side. This was not the kind of exchange she'd expected.

"It's not bad blood. It's just that you have a gift of getting on my nerves. You were always in my way, Duran. I put up with it for more than ten years when we were kids."

The easy, lighthearted cast to his face disappeared at her words, changing to a more deflated look. "It was never my intention to get in your way or on your nerves. I was just trying to be friendly."

They had been rivals, competitors, sparring partners. Never friends.

There had always been a line between them, an invisible axis, that bisected the world. One could never share with the other.

"You came back home like some kind of conquering hero," she declared, rising to her feet. Sitting behind the desk felt suffocating all of a sudden. She made her way around and sat at the edge of her table, biding her time to organize her thoughts. "Everyone in town has been talking about your Transcription Tower, how many jobs it would create, how a son of Iloilo never forgot his roots while he was making waves in the BPO industry. What was I supposed to think when you walked into the gym four days ago?"

"That I suck at Judo now?" he offered.

"That you came to gloat." Somehow, she felt defeated, drained, as soon as she said it.

"Gloat?" Royce walked further into the faculty room. His presence seemed to dwarf everything else in sight. He stopped a few feet in front of her. "That was the last thing on my mind, Koreen. Why would I gloat about anything, especially to you, of all people?"

She averted her eyes from his. *To make me feel as inconsequential as you always have.* She wanted to say it, so badly, but stopped herself. Instead, she listened to her own intakes of breath, to him breathing a short distance away. She could have sworn she could hear his heart pounding, or maybe it was her own. She wasn't sure of anything at that point.

"Koreen," he finally said. "Please look at me."

She did, not without hesitation. His dark eyes were laser-focused and unblinking against her own. "What?"

"I wanted to see you. When I found out you were still in town, I thought right away you would be the best person to run the Transcription Tower. I wanted to offer you a stake in the business."

This, she thought dazedly. This was the last thing she had ever expected him to say.

By far, it was the biggest possible shock he could have sprung on her. So much so, that all she could do was stare at him, dumbstruck.

"What made you think that?" she asked finally, carefully. "After all this time, you thought of me?"

He shrugged. "If I had to choose someone to trust my dreams and lifeblood with, it would be the smartest, hardest working and scariest person I know. You."

She had to shake her head. "You're crazy."

"There's no one like you, Koreen. Let me make that very clear. This is why I wanted to offer you partnership in our venture. I was going to tell you tonight, over dinner, under circumstances better than this."

For the longest time, and she could never really fathom how long, they both stood in the middle of the faculty room, wordlessly sizing each other up.

So this is how it feels to have your world turned upside down.

"I need some time to think about it," she heard herself say, after what seemed like the longest pause. "If that's what you're really asking."

"Yes, it is. Take all the time you need. I will arrange for the operations team in HQ to send you whatever you wish to know."

"Great." It was her turn to approach him. They were almost toe to toe when she stopped and looked him straight in the eye. "I have a class until nine o'clock tonight. What about dinner after?"

He was not the only one who could spring surprises.

The grin was back on his face in no time. "Dinner after."

THE SEDAN HE BORROWED FROM HIS FATHER PULLED UP THE CURB at exactly nine in the evening. From behind the wheel, Royce looked at the flight of stairs leading up to the gymnasium. Koreen's class was probably just wrapping up. He could wait.

It was strange, how quickly things could change. His seven years in Saudi Arabia had been a blur of endless work, fueled by a deep-rooted determination to bring a dream to life. The prince had repeatedly asked him to take a break: be with his family in the Philippines, find a wife, or simply take his mother and father on vacation. None of these mattered very much when Royce had his eyes on a goal.

Jeddah, Dubai, Pune, finally Iloilo. *Home*, where he was going to build a state-of-the-art transcription facility, possibly the biggest in Southeast Asia, and employ hundreds of his own countrymen.

Royce had come full circle.

It felt like he was back at the beginning, in some ways. A time in his life when all he wanted to do was impress the girl with the cat-like eyes. No matter what he did back then, she had always come out the smarter one in school, the one better prepared in projects and competitions, the one who could execute advanced Judo moves with the quiet strength and deadly precision of a born master.

Who could blame a man for trying then, and for trying again now?

When he found out she was still single, it was all he could do to stop himself from kissing and doing other things to her in the middle of their old Judo gym, when he first saw her. Besides, if he'd tried anything, he would have been in the hospital right now, if he was lucky.

For now, he took comfort and assurance that he had made his offer clear and, at the same time, stopped pissing her off so much by making her understand how he actually thought of her.

As far as back as he could remember, he had always held Koreen Cisco in the highest regard. Hell, he would build a pedestal for her, if she asked nicely, or maybe twisted his arm a little bit. It wouldn't take much.

"Ouch." The woman he couldn't stop thinking about materialized from the semi-darkness outside the car, pulling open the passenger door and unceremoniously sliding into the seat beside him. "The hips are hurting, and they never lie. Remind me, Duran, how are old are we?"

"Thirty-two."

"Numbers could hurt so much," she declared, lowering a large purple backpack to the car floor next to her feet. "That's something they don't put in the math textbooks."

"Good evening to you, too, Sensei." He could not help but admire how good she looked in the tie-dyed shift she was wearing. It was green and brown, setting off her red-gold skin tone perfectly. The yellow-orange light of the car interior gave her a luminous aura.

"I'm sorry to have kept you waiting," she said, turning her full attention to him. He noticed that she had put on makeup, making her unforgettable eyes look even more feline than they already were. "I didn't want to look like a sack of charcoal. A judo-gi could only get me so far."

"You look beautiful," he said. Unable to resist, he leaned over and gave her a peck on the cheek. "Thanks for accepting my invitation."

He braced himself for her reaction. A well-placed slap across the face or a punch in the gut, perhaps. He was willing to sacrifice a few teeth or have a few ribs broken.

Instead, she put a hand on his shoulder, just as he was pulling away from her, effectively stopping him.

"You're welcome," she replied, before pulling him back in.

This time it was her turn to press her lips to his cheek, her mouth lingering for several long, sweet seconds.

She reached for the spot she had just kissed, her fingers slowly dragging over his skin. It took a few seconds for him to realize she was removing traces of her lipstick.

"I'm starving, Duran. Let's go."

SHE SIPPED THE LAST FEW DROPS OF HER COFFEE, TAKING IN THE sight of him seated across from her at the table. All evening long, Royce had been relaxed and attentive, and so effortlessly funny. She had never really seen him that way before. Then again, she had never really spent any time with him in the past.

"I've never eaten so much in years," she said. "Thanks again."

He shook his head. "I had an ulterior motive, as I said earlier. But you're welcome. I'm glad we didn't have to talk business tonight."

She had to agree. 'Business' did not seem a suitable topic of conversation in a place like this. They were seated outdoors at a table of the hotel's poolside restaurant. Strains of music filtered out from the nearby ballroom. The sky was generously dotted with stars. The moon looked very pretty in its first quarter. The night breeze whipped Koreen's hair and caressed her skin. Through a half-stupor caused by roast beef, red wine and chocolate mousse, she had to admit the place felt very romantic.

Over the past several hours, she thought about what he had said at the faculty room that afternoon.

If I had to choose someone to trust my dreams and lifeblood with, it would be the smartest, hardest working and scariest person I know. You.

She felt surprised and amused, but, mostly, incredibly flattered. His offer was something she was definitely considering. Being a Mathematics and Judo teacher was not her endgame.

There was something else, gnawing at the periphery of her thoughts.

He had chosen her. He trusted her with his dreams and his lifeblood.

Royce Duran didn't seem the kind of man who carelessly threw words around.

Did he think *more* of her?

She tested that theory earlier, after he had kissed her for the first time in all the years they had known each other. She kissed him, too.

Her only indisputable conclusion was that she wanted more of it all. She wanted more of him.

She did not want what he had, not really. She had never wanted to have his charisma or his leadership skills or his athleticism.

The realization hit her like a tidal wave.

She wanted him.

The coffee cup, mercifully empty, slid from her grasp, landing on the green turf under her feet. The dancing varicolored lights surrounding the hotel pool gave her a sense of vertigo.

"Koreen?" He was beside her in an instant, on bended knee, concern written all over his face. "Are you alright?"

She felt heat suffuse her cheeks. Her throat suddenly felt very dry. She swallowed and nodded. "I'm fine. I think I need to get out of here."

"Of course." He stood up and reached for his card inside the billfold. He had paid for the entire meal and given a tip. The numbers on the tiny piece of paper inside the billfold were so offensive, she did not even dare glance a second time. "You must be tired. Let me take you home."

Her hand shot out, landing on his forearm. "I don't want to go home. Not yet. I never knew you were such a good loser. I want to find out more."

That was the best way of putting it.

Royce reached for her hands and helped her to her feet. His eyes were glued to her face, in what looked like a combination of fascination and surprise. She stared right back. She did not stop him when he pulled her close.

She did not stop herself, either, when she reached out and put her hands on his chest. Underneath her palms, she could feel his heartbeat, his breathing, and his body heat.

"What do you want to find out?" he asked softly.

The invisible line between them held, barely. If only she had the strength to break it.

"If you can lose in dancing, too."

It was two in the morning when they left the dance club of the hotel.

Royce parked the car in front of the gate as Koreen had directed. Behind the wrought-iron front entrance and concrete fence was a well-maintained two-story house, cream-colored under the streetlights, with large glass windows. He switched off the engine and turned on the car's overhead lights.

"My mother must think you kidnapped me or something," she said, rummaging through her handbag. "Can't imagine all her questions tomorrow morning. The perks of living with one's parents." She wrinkled her nose and feigned a shudder.

He remembered Koreen's parents very well. Her father was an architect, her mother a university professor. They had always treated him kindly, ever since he and Koreen were children. Her little brother, Kenneth, now a doctor in Family Medicine and completing residency in another province, was an old basketball buddy and, presently, a source of information on his sister's whereabouts (predictable) and relationships (non-existent).

His parents, on the other hand, adored Koreen. His father seemed to root more for her than for him, especially in Judo. His mother would always remind him to "go easy on the girl" or "keep an eye out for her."

Royce watched Koreen pull out her keys from the depths of her handbag. "The first time I had breakfast back home last week, I never realized how much food my mother used to make me eat. When I asked for coffee, she nearly threw me out of the house. She always thought coffee would stunt my growth."

"She's right, though. Looks like you listened when you were growing up." She laughed. "I would be happy to give her free one-on-one lessons on throwing, on the condition that she only applies her techniques on you."

"I wouldn't be surprised if she accepts, now that I'm around to actually throw."

"All my money's on her. She'll outrank you in no time."

They sat in companionable silence, her keys dangling in her hand. He didn't make a move to relieve her of them, as a gentleman was supposed to do.

He didn't want the night to end. He still carried a vivid mental picture of Koreen dancing in his arms. She had been like a firefly the entire evening, generating energy all over the place. For probably the first time in their lives, they had done something together where they did not compete or keep score. They had just danced, plain and simple.

"Are you here to stay, Royce?"

Coming from her lips, his first name sounded foreign to his own ears. It was the first time she had called him that way. As far as he could remember, she had addressed him by his family name.

"You can say that, for the next few years at least," he replied. "I have to get permits and then start construction. After that, it's going to be a lot of work outfitting the Tower. I'll need to start recruiting a core launch group in the next month or so. I would have to travel back to Saudi later this year, to keep my visa valid. There are other sites to visit as well."

"Sounds very busy," she commented. "As promised, I'll think about your offer. It's too good to pass up, to be honest."

There was a change in her tone of voice. He searched her face. Still flushed from her night out, her skin almost glowed. "Please do. I'll be waiting for your answer."

He watched her shoulders rise and fall as she took a few deep breaths. "Well, thank you for the wonderful evening. I had a great time. I have never had this much fun since...I don't know. Maybe I've never had this much fun before." She shrugged and made a move to reach for her purple backpack.

It was his turn to stop her. "Koreen."

She paused mid-gesture, her cat-like eyes meeting his. "Yes?"

"Do you think we could be friends now? Start over?"

She picked up her backpack and slung it over her shoulder. "I'd like that," she answered, opening the door on her side of the car. She was on the pavement before he could ask anything else. "Good night, Duran." The passenger door shut in his face.

Why he had to be so obsessed with this woman, in the way he was right now, he had no idea.

"Wait." Fumbling a bit with his own door, he half-stumbled out of the car and made his way to her, catching up as she reached a small side gate.

"Koreen," he repeated.

"What?" Frustration was clear in her voice. The keys in her hand jangled loudly as she tried to unlock the gate. It didn't open.

It took him a second to see the reason for her failure. Her hands were shaking.

It took him one stride to get to her. He didn't take the keys from her hand, as a gentleman should.

He took her in his arms, brought his lips down to hers, and kissed her.

He was ready to lose. Lose his teeth, his bones, and, if she wanted, his heart.

Always unwilling to be outdone, she kissed him back. Just as a cat would, her arms and legs went around him tightly, possessively, marking her territory. He gladly took her weight, absorbing every bit of the heaven that was her and her touch.

When they finally pulled apart, panting, he was the first to speak. He didn't let her go. If she wanted him to, he would. But not yet.

"I'm sorry," he whispered into her hair.

Koreen was leaning against him, her head on his shoulder,

her feet barely touching the ground. Her arms were still around his torso. She was breathing heavily.

"Are you?" She looked up at him, eyes blazing. "You're sorry for this?"

"No, I'll never be sorry for any of this." Unable to stop himself, he reached for her hair. The strands felt like silk on his fingers. Touching her was something he could get used to. "I'm sorry if this isn't what you want."

"I've wanted this for the longest time." She followed suit, reaching for his face, tugging at his hair.

Encouraged by her answer, he put his arms around her waist, pulling her even closer. "I didn't know what you wanted, Koreen. All you had to do was tell me."

"I think I did more than just tell you." Her fingers framed his face, holding him in place. "And you? What do you want, Royce?"

"I've wanted to impress a girl ever since we were children. I had to make sure she noticed me, but I was nothing compared to her. She is the smartest, strongest and scariest person I know."

"She doesn't think you're nothing," Koreen replied, smiling. "She thinks you're everything she has ever wanted, too."

He smiled back, his heart now in her hands. "If she wants me, I'm all hers."

"Good." She put her arms around his neck. It felt like a submission headlock and an embrace at the same time. "Now impress her."

"Now we're talking." He went in for another kiss, and maybe another one after that.

Koreen allowed herself to drown in him.

There was nothing to resist, measure or control. There was

only the feeling of his arms around her, his lips on hers, his voice in her ear.

There was only a sense of triumph that, yes, he belonged to her, and she to him.

In the darkest hours of dawn, she felt the invisible line between them melt away, as if it was never there.

Dancing in the Rain

DANCING IN THE RAIN

He had fallen hard and fast.
She had not been of any help, either. She had wanted him, too.

At the end of the night they first danced, she had taken his hand, led him to the darkened, empty backstage area of the auditorium, and kissed him.

He had kissed her back, among other things.

She was his first, in so many ways.

Foreword

This piece of short fiction was first printed in the literary folio *The Accounts: Initial Public Offerings* of the University of the Philippines-Visayas, College of Management, Iloilo City.

At the time of its initial publication, *'Dancing in the Rain'* broke the idea of the typical college romance, turning tropes on their head.

In 2023, I decided to revisit and rewrite it into a novella for my birthday. It had since taken the form of the novella *Shadow and Light* (September 2023).

THE STORY

Dancing in the Rain

THE DEN

Morning came with a howling wind, the kind that carried dirt and muck that stuck on the skin and never washed out. It seemed to scream in pain.

Arthur gritted his teeth. The storm was over but everything in the campus was still drenched. He knew it would be very cold on the field, not to mention muddy. The football pitch looked more like a swamp when he passed it on the way to the college's main building.

Coach wanted them to start putting in more hours *now*, before first period, for the citywide inter-collegiate tournament opening game next week. Come rain or flood or any other calamity, they would defend their title all the way up to regionals, for the second year in a row.

He descended the steps to the building's basement. It was only six-thirty. The prized player's first class started at eight and now he was most probably in his lair, practicing those deft knee tricks that brought tears to the eyes of the rival coaches.

As team captain, it was Arthur's job to secure the gear and inform the prized player about that morning's practice not getting cancelled in spite of the field's condition.

Not that he'd care either way, he thought bitterly

The prized player was a tireless machine, not a person. He'd show up, do the drills and rounds, and commit the plays to memory. Arthur often wondered what possessed him to turn down the position of captain, after bringing the team to two regional championships since he was a freshman.

Even as a senior, Arthur was only the distant second choice to lead the team this year. His numbers in goals and successful plays were pathetic compared to the prized player's, as was everyone else's. The man pretty much did not miss goals.

He typed in the door code and stepped inside the basement, which housed a collection of old school furniture and relatively new sports equipment. He knocked on the door of a smaller room inside, once a storage closet for cleaning equipment and break room for campus cleaning staff, before the lay-offs. This was now the prized player's residence on campus, because he didn't want to share his space with three other kids in the dormitory next door.

No answer. Arthur turned the knob, finding it unlocked, and pushed warily.

There was nothing in the prized player's room except a sparse wooden cot, an equally drab three-legged table and a portable clothes rack.

The team helped him load back the equipment only last night, he thought. *Knowing him, he wouldn't move out of this place. It's his lion's den, after all.*

Arthur knew that the prized player had some other stuff around, like dartboards, target posters, and sketches of exotic birds. They were all gone. Nothing was draped on the makeshift clothesline strung across the tiny room.

He stood there and assessed this new information for half a minute.

Arthur took a deep breath and closed the door. He retraced his steps in the basement, retrieving two footballs from the storage racks before he left.

He had better tell Coach that Aragon was gone.

THE DARK
Dawn.

He gingerly lowered his body onto the lopsided stone bench overlooking the quad. His muscles ached and his sides burned from the run.

The campus was still cloaked in darkness. He had been running for more than an hour, but the sky still resembled a blue-black canopy strewn with darker masses of clouds. Not a ray of sunlight breached his limited view of the horizon. The air was thick and heavy, and sullied by city dust.

Rain was coming.

He felt a detached, perverse satisfaction.

"Aragon?"

A female voice had said his family name. People knew him by that name.

Aragon. A name full of history. His place of birth was far enough away, but he could still recollect the smells of gunpowder, the crisp click of a gun's hammer, the echo of death cries. They all came with his heritage.

His well-trained eyes made out her silhouette. The lighting in the campus was limited and the few functional lampposts badly needed their bulbs replaced.

"Jerann." Her name fell from his lips. After all this time, he was still surprised at the way he would say it. Softer, slower than his usual speech, and always with awe.

She was dressed in a white top with her jean shorts. The wind played with the strands of her long hair. She carried a black duffel bag, the size of which dwarfed her frame.

He wasn't surprised to feel his chest tighten, his heartbeat accelerate. "What are you doing here? How did you get in the campus?"

He watched her place the bag on the concrete pavement and take a seat beside him. Her eyes, always strangely luminous, flickered in the semi-darkness.

"I had to see you," she replied simply.

"How did you get in?" he pressed.

He lived on campus, in the main building's basement. He had first lodged in a boarding house, then moved to the dormitory after he secured a permanent spot in the college's varsity football team. He hated the noise and the activity of shared living spaces.

Coach had allowed him to hole up in the old janitors' break room, right next to the storage where sports teams kept all their equipment. The older man could not refuse the simple request of the college's star athlete and pulled every string he could with administration to make this strange request happen.

"The fence is only about seven feet, max." There was a smile in her voice. "I couldn't sleep. I figured you would be here."

"Yes. I couldn't sleep either. As always, the best option is to run."

He opened his arms and she snuggled into them. She pressed her face to his chest, not minding his sweat-soaked shirt.

"You should eat more," she said.

"Really?"

"Yes. I don't know where you get all that energy to move so

fast, or to kick that hard." Her breath whispered through the worn material of his shirt. "Or to run so much every day."

"I don't know. Habit, maybe."

They both lapsed into silence. In the darkness, she reached for his hands. He felt her delicate skin brush against his scarred and callused palms. Even though they were much, much closer than people expected them to be, he had never once stopped marveling at how he and Jerann appeared to be so different from each other.

She was the epitome of intelligence and charisma. Everyone liked her – from the teachers, to the cafeteria staff, even the freshmen and the super-seniors. She always had that ready smile and the time to listen to everyone's problems. People believed that sleeping wasn't on her busy schedule, that Jerann Castelo would rather stay up talking to someone in her trademark high-octane and witty manner, organizing events as a member of the Supreme Student Council, or tutoring younger students in Calculus.

He was popular in another fashion: the star football player who never gave away much about himself. The name Aragon struck fear in the varsity teams of colleges all over the region. Ever since his freshman year, he had brought the university an unprecedented steady stream of championships.

He was not, however, raised to become an athletic achiever. His training had aimed to accomplish more serious ends.

Deadly serious ends.

In his first year, their class had gone on a trip up the mountains as part of their Biology subject. While everyone had lugged bags of canned goods and other packaged foods, he had only brought clothes and minimal camping equipment. Evening at their campsite, the teacher had asked, "Where's the dinner you're supposed to bring for yourself?"

"It's right behind you, sir." He had thrown his hunting knife, the blade whizzing a mere inch above his professor's head.

A wild chicken, an *ilahas*, had squawked and crashed to the ground in rapid succession. He then had an entire roasted chicken for his dinner, served hot. No one had shared his meal, or had spoken to him for the rest of the trip. The teacher gave him a grade of 1.0.

After that, everyone dealt with him very cautiously. No one dared to test his temper, even though he had never once displayed it, on or off the field.

He liked things that way. The further he distanced himself, the better.

Only Jerann had dared break through that wall between him and the rest of the world. During the college mixer party at the start of their sophomore year, she had asked him to dance, locating him in the shadows of the auditorium. He had been standing in a corner, nearly undetectable as far as he was concerned. He was fond of honing his stealth skills, but she had made him realize his abilities at the time were rather rusty, if not questionable.

Jerann Castelo, one of the most popular girls in school, was actually standing right there and asking him to dance with her.

The varicolored strobe lights of the darkened building had accentuated the spark of recklessness in her eyes.

He had been very flustered. "I don't know how to–"

"Aragon, if you turn me down, I will kill you."

In that very moment, he fell in love with her.

THE CONFESSION

That was more than a year ago.

He had fallen hard and fast.

She had not been of any help, either. She had wanted him, too.

At the end of the night they first danced, she had taken his hand, led him to the darkened, empty backstage area of the auditorium, and kissed him.

He had kissed her back, among other things. He had tried to find his way through their sweaty clothing and bodies, her scent of cologne, something fruity and warm, undeniably overpowering his reason and control. She had tasted of something fruity and warm, too, all of her.

Since then, he had been unable to distance himself or stop thinking about her, no matter how hard he tried.

She had been his first, in so many ways.

Nobody knew anything about what went on between them. It had been a perfectly hidden secret, until the time Lexie, Jerann's best friend, had seen them kissing in an empty classroom before the citywide football championship last year.

But whatever Lexie saw was never mentioned. He understood why she and Jerann were best friends; they kept each other's secrets without question.

"The first time I saw you, you were practicing alone in the field," Jerann was now saying. "You never missed a shot at the goal. You were wearing this exact same shirt. It was kind of new then."

He smiled in the darkness. Only very few had seen him smile.

She felt the slight chuckle rumbling through his chest. "What the hell are you so amused about?"

"You." He pulled her closer. Jerann's frame fitted his bigger one snugly. "Why do you always have to be so *perfect*? You remember, know, and do almost everything."

Her breathing seemed to stop. It took moments before she could answer. "I was raised to be like that, as an only child. No one could make up for my mistakes, if I was stupid enough to make them. That was my first lesson in life."

She paused, as if gathering momentum. "When I was little, they had my tutor slap my hands with a stick when I couldn't spell a word correctly. Or sometimes they wouldn't let me have dinner unless I could recite an entire declamation speech without any mistakes. I got good at all of it. Then better. By the time I was eight, there was no more need for such discipline. I delivered everything they wanted."

The words had a bitter edge. He could taste them in his own heart. If there was someone who understood, only too well, how it was like to rise to the nearly impossible expectations and demands of their family, it was him.

"It gets exhausting. I'm doing a great job at it, though. There are so many people expecting so many things. I had to do all those things. I feel guilty when I couldn't. Sometimes it's like digging your own grave. But you feel the need to do it anyway." Her voice sounded rough and strained. "At some point, the need becomes a want. It becomes part of you, killing you like some kind of cancer."

The first few raindrops fell. He felt them on his arm. Then he realized they weren't from the sky. The droplets were her tears. In all the time he had known Jerann, this was the first time he had seen her cry.

Something bubbled inside him. It wasn't rage, but a calmer desire to kill. It was part of him, his lifeblood. Although he had vowed to himself never to take a human life again, he would break that for her in a heartbeat. He would murder anyone in cold blood to spare her from getting hurt.

But there was no one entirely responsible for that sort of torment she felt. Just like no one had to pay for his past, except perhaps he himself.

"I'm sorry..." His voice trailed off. He felt lame and helpless, as the familiar cold numbness ran the length of his spine. It was a feeling only pulling the trigger could relieve. "I shouldn't have said–"

"It's not your fault. Sometimes I just couldn't help remembering things like that." She bravely swallowed back her sobs.

He gently wiped her tears away, careful so his rough skin would not scratch her face. "I had it coming. I had it coming all these years. It was only a matter of time before I burnt out."

He waited for her to calm down. She could so easily collect herself, or at least appear to have done so. He was the only one who would always know and feel the trembling of her hands, the uneven beating of her pulse, even if she appeared perfectly composed.

She had looked like this during debates when she ran for the student council, when after she felt as cold as ice to his touch. Everyone else had praised her composure and quick thinking, never considering the amount of control it took on her part.

"I was raised to be the best, too," he said, slowly, cautiously. "I became the best."

Jerann's tearstained face had a look that showed the struggle to comprehend his words. She said nothing, but spoke volumes with wide eyes.

He knew at that point he had to explain, to make her understand.

"When I was in high school, I was known as Cain in the underground. My father chose that name for me. I was born with a twin brother, but my cord was around his neck when we were cut out...I choked him to death in our mother's womb."

"I didn't know..." She was groping for words. "You never-"

He squeezed her hands in his, shaking his head slightly, feeling his lips turn in that slight, almost imperceptible smile he could give to no one but her.

It was his way of telling her it was okay. He would be okay, if he had her with him.

"I'm the youngest of four brothers, but I could outshoot all of them. I could take them all down hand to hand, too, by the time I was seven. I was faster and stronger. I was even better in most sports. A lot of schools offered everything from bribes to scholarship packages to my parents so I would go to their place, just so they could get all the football titles, even a national games medal."

"My father then told us that the mantle of the Eagle-Eye had to be passed down. He was almost sixty and it was about time for him to mentor the next one. All my uncles – everyone in my family - wanted me to take it. I was fourteen. The Eagle-Eye tattoo meant the world."

"That explains the eagle mark on your chest." Jerann placed her hand over his heart. "It's more than just a tattoo."

"Our family has been in the Philippines for more than three hundred years. You can say we wrote a lot of history in blood and no one ever knew. We are loyal to no one, except our own kin and land. That's how we had roots. The Eagle-Eye is the best of the present generation. He was entrusted to carry out the most dangerous missions."

He said everything without any pride. Then again, there was nothing to be proud of.

A series of frozen frames flashed in his memory. He drew in a sharp breath at how vividly he could remember the events of six years past.

"My initiation rite was to kill a priest who had sexually abused the son of one of our workers at the corn farm. The boy was eight, a *sacristan*. It was three-thirty in the morning...the priest was walking to Church to prepare for the *misa de gallo*. I got him with one shot, right between the eyes. It was Christmas when I became the ninth-generation Eagle-Eye. That's when I got the tattoo. 'You will be Cain now,' my father said."

"There are twenty-seven others on my list; two of them were very young, maybe five or six years old. They were the children of a drug lord who thought he could smuggle *shabu* through one of the canning companies in town. They saw me shoot their father. *Leave no witnesses.* That was in the rules."

"You killed people." Her voice was toneless. Not angry, afraid or accusing, just clear and audible.

"I left Surallah thinking I could somehow lose that part of me. I bargained for four years to finish school so there's time to think about it. No matter how hard you try, that side of you stays right where it is. If you try to get rid of it somehow, it will eat you up alive. You could shed your skin, but not your blood. You wouldn't have the strength to survive."

He realized she had not backed away, or showed any sign of fear or disgust. Before he could say anything more, she looked straight into his eyes, unblinking. He could see clarity in her gaze, behind the sheen of dried tears and in the soft light of the oncoming sunrise. The clarity that his pain was hers, too.

"I love you, Nick. Nothing can change that."

Nick.

His Christian name was Nicholas, but no one called him that. It was always Aragon to everybody else. Only Jerann called him by his first name.

He swallowed hard, completely mesmerized. "I should have told you. I'm so sorry-"

"There's nothing to be sorry about." Her voice rang with certainty. "You may be an assassin, you may be the most feared killer in the whole world, but I love you for what you are. I found in you a part of myself that I thought I would never find in anyone else. Don't you know how good it feels to finally hear you talk about your past?"

She stood up and put her arms around him. She then took a step back and placed a hand on her own belly. "I love you for being the father of this child."

It took a second for him to understand what she meant by both her actions and words. When he finally did, he felt all the air leave his lungs.

He could only stare at her, speechless, as a sudden glow

began to form in the pit of his stomach. It was a warmth he had known only when he met her.

When he could finally muster some kind of self-control, he said, "You are..." His voice trailed off. It was difficult to put into words.

She smiled. "Maybe six weeks now. A doctor who doesn't know my family confirmed it yesterday afternoon. That's why I had to see you. I could no longer keep this a secret." She clutched at his shoulders. Her face, so breathtakingly beautiful to him, was a study of mixed emotions. "I had to tell you."

"I'm going to be a father," he said slowly, tasting the word. He put his hands on her stomach, above her own. His own blood, with hers.

Father, he repeated inwardly. Not a mentor or a predecessor. A father.

She nodded. "And I'm going to have this baby. *Our child.*"

This time, the first real drops of rain started to fall.

A droplet landed on his lips. He tasted sweetness and warmth. It bore none of the bitter taste and spilled blood of the past three hundred years. A bolt of lightning streaked across the sky, followed by a loud rumble of thunder, just before the downpour came down in earnest.

By silent mutual agreement, neither of them suggested taking shelter in the nearby gazebos surrounding the campus quad.

Jerann stepped back and spread out her arms, giggling as she turned her face up to the downpour.

As he watched her spinning in the rain, he realized that he was still half-stunned by her news.

"Nick, come with me," she said. "I want to dance with you."

In that moment, his head cleared, as if someone had shone a light on the shadows of his burden. He stood up and took her hands. "I love you. We will have our child."

She smiled and stood on tiptoes, pressing her lips to his. "I would never have it any other way."

He placed her palms over his heart, on the very same spot where his body bore the Eagle-Eye mark. "That is my vow."

She reached up and touched his cheek. "For the first time in our lives, let's not be the perfect killer or the perfect girl. Let's do the right thing and just be us."

"Yes." He put his hand over hers and kissed her fingers. "Us," he repeated, trying the sound of the word rolling off his tongue. He realized he liked it.

The rain fell harder.

He basked in the sight of the woman who had looked him in the eye and never crumbled, even after his confession and the deaths he had brought.

Instead, she embraced him and his blood.

She was looking straight back at him, the way she had the night they first danced. The night she opened the door to his heart and, unwittingly, to his freedom from the shadows of the past.

Nicholas Aragon embraced her then.

Nothing more was said. The rain crashed around them, drenching concrete, earth, galvanized iron and their bodies.

When the sun finally rose, the thunderstorm came to an end. Only the wind was left howling, singing a dirge to the shadows as they became one with the light.

THE LETTER

Lexie worked for the campus publication. It was her habit for the past two years to drop by the newspaper office every morning to check on messages and writing assignments.

When she arrived, on the dot, at half-past seven, the first thing she noticed was a folded note tacked to the door corkboard. Her name was on it, in a familiar roundish script.

She took the paper off the board and unlocked the newspaper office.

The note felt slightly damp in her hands as she unfolded it. The paper seemed to have gotten wet in the rain earlier that morning and was slowly drying out.

> *My dearest Lexie,*
> *I've held on for years to who I thought I was.*
> *I have become the perfect puppet to expectations that were never mine. It's time to cut the strings.*
> *I gave them my entire life until now. From today, it's my turn to live the rest of it on my own terms.*
> *I will miss you.*
> *Love always,*
> *Jeri*

She stared at the signature. Like her best friend's personality, it had an undeniable, inimitable flourish.

For a long time, Lexie stood in the middle of the empty office, her gaze seeing beyond the unlit space before her.

It wasn't a matter of why, she thought. *But a matter of when.*

She went through the publication's memo slips on the assignment board, locked the office, and headed to her first class of the day.

Along the way, she stopped by one of the trash cans on the quad and tore the letter to shreds. She watched the tiny white pieces fall from her hands like raindrops disappearing into the cold morning air.

"Be happy, Jeri," Lexie whispered. "I'll miss you, too."

About The Author

Shirley Siaton writes edgy and evocative novels and poems. Her worlds are in a deliciously dark cross-section of the romance, neo-noir, action, fantasy, new adult, and contemporary genres.

She has several books of fiction and poetry released since February 2023. Her first book is the free verse collection *'Black Cat and other poems.'* She also pens juvenile literature as Shirley Parabia.

She is an award-winning writer, poet, and journalist in English, Filipino, and Hiligaynon, lauded by the Stevan Javellana Foundation, Philippine Information Agency, and West Visayas State University. Her essays, short stories, and poems have been published internationally in print and digital media. Her multilingual plays have been staged in the Philippines.

Shirley is a black belt in Shotokan Karate and an international certified fitness coach. She has a Master's degree in Public Administration and a career in international education. Originally from Iloilo City, she lives in the Middle East with her husband and two daughters.

On The Web

Shirley's official website:
shirleysiaton.com

Complete reading guide:
shirley.pub

Subscribe to Shirley's VIP list for free exclusive updates:
newsletter.shirleysiaton.com

www.ingramcontent.com/pod-product-compliance
Lightning Source LLC
LaVergne TN
LVHW011047100526
838202LV00078B/3833